Six Tales for Nephews and Nieces

and other picture- stories

Wilhelm Busch　著

陸谷孫　譯

三民

© 非尋常童話
Six Tales for Nephews and Nieces

著作人	Wilhelm Busch
譯 者	陸谷孫
發行人	劉振強
著作財 產權人	三民書局股份有限公司
	臺北市復興北路三八六號
發行所	三民書局股份有限公司
	地 址／臺北市復興北路三八六號
	郵 撥／〇〇〇九九九八一五號
印刷所	三民書局股份有限公司
門市部	復北店／臺北市復興北路三八六號
	重南店／臺北市重慶南路一段六十一號
初 版	中華民國八十五年三月

編 號 S 88002

基本定價 肆元

行政院新聞局登記證局版臺業字第〇二〇〇號

有著作權·不准侵害

ISBN　957-14-2455-2 （精裝）

©by Verlag Johannes Heyn, Klagenfurt, Austria, 1992

©for exclusive Chinese language and English-Chinese languages

by San　Min Book Co., Ltd., Taipei, Taiwan, 1995

維爾翰‧布希小傳
(WILHELM BUSCH)

　　維爾翰‧布希(WILHELM BUSCH)為一德國畫家和作家，1832年四月十五日生於 Wiedensahl（位於漢諾瓦），1908 年一月九日歿於 Mechtshausen。曾參加杜塞道夫(Dusseldorf)、安特衛普(Antwerpen)及慕尼黑(Munchen)協會，1898年退休。維爾翰‧布希為德國通俗幽默作家，其影響在於他能準確的結合滑稽、簡單的雙行押韻詩，和尖銳、簡明的插圖。他的畫風也頗具諷刺性，處理畫作時，喜揭穿自以為是、假道學和虛偽的虔誠。維爾翰‧布希亦創造了哲理性的抒情詩及散文，此方面是特別受到叔本華(Arthur Schopenhauer)的影響。

Index

The Rabbit

小兔

The rabbit in the cabbage sits,
Enjoys his snack in little bits.
A white dear lamb, which had no fear,
Was grazing in the field quite near.

小兔蹲在白菜地，
小口啃食好得意。
不知害怕的小白羊，
吃草近旁在田疆。

The wolf, so wicked and so grim,
Sneaked up and took the lamb with him.
The rabbit was a witness.

大灰狼，兇殘又陰刁，
偷偷上前把羊兒叼。
小兔在旁瞧。

Therefore it jumped and ran
Up to the farmer, thus began:
''Oh woe is me!
Please come and see!

小兔跳起急急跑，
去向農夫把訊報。
「喔，真叫人悲傷！
求你快去看一趟！

The wolf, so beastly and so grim,
Sneaked round and took the lamb with him!"

大灰狼，殘忍又陰刁，
偷偷叼去了小羊羔！」

The farmer Jack came up
And took his heavy club.
"Thank you", he said and chose

農夫傑克站起身，
一把抓起大木棍。
「多謝！」說著掄棍打，

To hit poor rabbit's nose.

"You will no longer steal my cabbage!"
The farmer laughed: "I'll stop your ravage!"

打中可憐小兔的鼻樑。

「看你再敢偷白菜！」
農夫哈哈說：「再敢來破壞！」

And those who cannot see world's habit
Will be as clever as the rabbit.

不識世事的糊塗蛋，
到頭來傻得跟小兔一般。

Good Mary

好瑪麗

There was a castle once, in which
A woman lived here proud and rich.

從前有座城堡，
住個富婆好驕傲。

In this poor cottage, you see here,
Lived Mary with her mother dear.
Poor mother who was ill indeed,
Has nothing she could drink or eat.

而在圖中的茅屋，
瑪麗和母親苦生活。
可憐媽媽臥病在床，
沒吃沒喝叫人心傷。

So Mary thought: "I will now run
Up to the castle, it's soon done!"

瑪麗心想：「我一溜小跑，
立刻可以趕到城堡！」

She took a slice of some stale bread,
For this was all they only had.
A bridge was crossing here the bog,
And there was sitting a poor dog.
"My master", cries the dog, "is dead,
Oh, had I but a piece of bread!"

她帶上一片走味的麵包，
這是全家僅剩的食料。
小橋橫跨沼地在這頭，
那邊躺著條可憐的狗。
「主人死了，」狗兒聲調悲，
「多想吃片麵包填我胃！」

Said Mary: "You are really slim",
Took out her bread, gave it to him.

瑪麗說：「你真瘦！」
掏出麵包便餵狗。

And while she ran on, stick in hand,
A fish was lying on the sand.

她拄著棍兒往前去，
忽見沙裡陷條魚。

"Oh", said the fish, my death is grim
Could I but in the water swim!"

「喔！」魚兒說，「死到臨頭，
多想回到水裡游一游！」

And Mary bending down she took
The fish back to the saving brook.

瑪麗俯身把魚抱，
放回小溪救了命一條。

Now to the castle, with great care,
She ran and found the woman there.

戰戰兢兢往前奔，
見到城堡女主人。

"Have mercy, madam", thus she prays,
"My mother's been ill for many days!"

「行行好，太太，」瑪麗哀聲求，
「我媽媽已經病了好久好久！」

"Away from here, you cheeky slut,
For such bad folk my door is shut!"

「滾開，你這不要臉的爛丫頭，
對你們這號人老娘從來不收留！」

Her eyes are filled with tears, you see,
And she sat down beneath a tree.

瑪麗兩眼淚汪汪，
坐在樹下暗神傷。

But hark, a tiny voice so clear
Came from the hollow tree quite near.
"Oh help me out, this is no fun,
What I want is to see the sun!"

A little hole, it was bad luck,
Is shut up with a tiny plug.

This plug was soon pulled out by her,
And Mary said: "Come out, dear sir!"

聽啊，近處有株空心樹，
樹幹傳出輕聲訴。
「喔，救我出去，這兒好難受，
重見天日我方有奔頭！」

倒霉一個小小洞口，
被木塞封得滴水不漏。

瑪麗拔出木塞打開洞：
「出來吧，樹精公公！」

But look, a snake from yonder tree
Crawled out and crept along with glee.
It coiled up tight, but was not wicked
And disappeared into the thicket.
It rustled there, but did not bite,
And with a flower out did glide.

誰知，瞧，樹洞爬出一條蛇，
曲曲彎彎游動得好抖擻。
蛇身緊盤但無惡意，
一會鑽沒在密林裡。
蛇不咬人，只是呼呼作聲，
過後送出鮮花一朵來謝恩。

Oh, flower, you with hope will fill
All people, who are badly ill.

And Mary took the magic flower,
It was indeed a blessed hour!

喔，花兒花兒多鮮美，
治病救人最顯威。

瑪麗取過魔法花，
真是老天睜眼救我媽！

But while she ran on her way back,
A robber stood there on the track.

瑪麗忙著跑回家，
不料強盜站在路上要搶她。

With terror she began to scream,
The flower fell into the stream.

驚惶失措放聲叫，
一不小心魔花往溪中掉。

The dog, however, grabbed the man
And chased him to the wood again.

狗兒跑來捉強盜，
把他追得直往樹林逃。

The fish is also helpful there
And brought the flower back to her.

魚兒也來幫一手，
啣起魔花送回她的手。

And Mary ran, with joy and cheer,
Home quickly to her mother dear.
The flower was of such a sort
That mother's health was soon restored.

喜氣洋洋開顏笑，
回家去問慈母好。
魔花果然有法力，
媽媽立時病除把床起。

By healing other people's need
Brought Mary happiness indeed.

別的病人她也醫，
見人康復最令瑪麗喜。

The wicked woman was, however,
Made by the robber dead for ever.

城堡富婆沒良心，
強盜刀下喪了命。

The Sack And The Mice

老鼠偷糧

A sack quite full of wheat and tall
Was standing proudly in the hall.
There came the cunning rout of mice,
Began to sing now in a trice:

小麥裝得袋兒飽，
放在屋裡衝天高。
狡猾老鼠偷糧來，
頓時喊喊喳喳嚷嚷開：

"You sack here on the wall,
Our lord we may you call!
Most thick you are and tight,
And so it's fully right
To pay you reverence,
Most mighty Excellence!"

「袋子靠牆根，
我們尊你叫大人。
袋兒大，袋兒滿，
我們自然不胡亂。
該敬禮處且敬禮，
我們向你獻敬意！」

The sack was proud and full of pleasure,
When it was honoured in such measure.

While it delighted in its role,
A mouse was gnawing it a hole.

袋子聞言喜不自勝，
誰曾給我這等尊稱。
這邊兀自得意洋洋，
那邊老鼠咬袋偷糧。

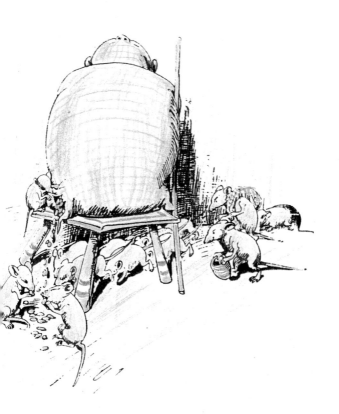

And while the corn was pouring out,
The mice were active without doubt.

麥粒麥粒滾於前，
鼠群奔忙不得閒。

The sack began to dwindle fast,
The mice became quite fat at last.

快快癟縮袋變小，
老鼠吃成大肥佬。

When emptied it was but a rag,
No one could recognize the sack.

糧去袋空，留下一方破布片，
飽滿不再，先前糧袋已不見。

At last they tore it from its throne
And left the useless sack alone.

鼠群咬扯破布片，
拖下寶座丟現眼。

While marching off they only spoke:
"Good-bye, farewell, Lord Stonybroke!"

列隊得勝班師去，
老鼠不忘齊聲噓：
「別了，你這顆粒不存的老大人！」

The Two Sisters

兩姐妹

Let me now of two sisters tell,
Whom I remember very well.
The name of one was Adelaide,
Coquetish, vain was she indeed.
The other with the name of Kate
Was diligent and a good maid.
She toiled all day, did seldom talk,
While Adelaide went for a walk.
Red wine was served for Adelaide,
While only water was for Kate.

故事在說姐妹倆，
我把它記得牢又詳。
姐姐名叫阿德萊，
虛榮而且好獻媚。
妹妹凱特好姑娘，
勤奮勞作責任強。
悠閒度日，阿德萊出門去散步，
從早到晚，凱特默默幹活不叫苦。
佳釀紅酒姐姐品，
留下粗茶妹妹飲。

One day they sent Kate to the grove
To get dry wood to heat the stove.

Quite near the pond, a frog
Was sitting on a block.
It croaked and wailed like mad
And felt indeed quite sad.
"Have mercy, see my wretched face,
Give me a kiss and an embrace!"

一天凱特被打發去森林，
為燃爐火拾柴薪。

溪邊石上蹲一蛙，
可憐巴巴叫呱呱。
「在我醜臉加一吻，
再來摟我親一親！」

So Katy thought: "It's just a jest
Or this poor frog will find no rest!"

That kiss is awful, it is true,
But look, the grassgreen frog turned blue.

凱特暗思忖:「青蛙在逗笑,
倘不吻抱牠會受不了。」

嘴唇貼上蛙皮真犯難,
怪的是青皮頓時變深藍。

The second kiss was not so bad,
The frog was growing now like mad.

第二吻更奇妙，
蛙體脹大又升高。

And at the third there was a flash,
As if a hundred cannons crash.

A castle grew above the moor,
A prince appeared then at the door.
He said: "I swear it on my knee,
My love and princess you shall be!"

And happy Katy, as is told,
Had robes embroidered now with gold.
And when she with her prince did sup,
Drank wine now from a golden cup.

第三吻引來電光閃,
似有百尊大砲齊參戰。

沼澤平地起城堡,
門口站一王子英武又年少。
王子說:「我來跪下發個誓,
娶你做王妃,愛你一輩子!」

傳說凱特聞言喜,
錦繡華服身上披。
她陪王子去進餐,
葡萄美酒盈金盞。

While this did happen, Adelaide
Went for a walk into the shade.
Quite near a pond among the brier,
There was a boy who had a lyre.
He plucked the strings and sang this ditty:
"Give me a kiss, you child, so pretty!"

話分兩頭說說阿德萊，
信步走進樹陰命多哀。
溪邊林中坐一美少年，
懷抱豎琴輕撥弦。
少年情歌順口溜：
「給我一吻，你這俊小妞！」

But from this kiss
She had no bliss,

The boy turned green,
icecold and mean,

殊不知這一吻，
吻出了禍事多多福無分。

少年搖身一變形：
青面獠牙，體膚冰冷。

And now, oh fright!
Became a nasty watersprite.

喔，真個嚇死人，
原來是個兇殘水妖精。

"Ha - ha", he laughed, "you are now bound
To come with me deep in the ground!"

「哈 — 哈」，妖精笑，

「定要你跟老子河底去逍遙！」

She sat among the water-rats,
The sprite's bald head she had to scratch.
She wore a dress of mossy rush,
And what she ate was muddy slush.
And when she wished a drop to drink,
Was water there up to the brink.

水底河鼠成了堆，
侍候禿頭妖精苦難挨。
青苔成衣難蔽體，
吞下泥沙權充飢。
唯有一件可不愁，
河水解渴管她夠。

Little Tom Thumb

拇指「湯姆」

A little tailor, slim and skinny,
Lived with his wife, whose name was Winnie.
They also had a little boy,
So small in height just like a toy.
He was not bigger than a plum,
And just as long as here my thumb.

Because he was so wee and slim,
Tom Thumb became the name for him.
But courage he had like a lord,
Sharp like a needle was his sword;
With it he had in one short breath
Three flies stabbed thoroughly to death.

This done he had a little doze,
Flat on his tummy and his nose.

瘦骨伶仃小裁縫，
娶來溫妮倒鸞鳳。
生下小兒家添丁，
身高猶如玩具兵。
個頭大小像顆李，
長度只跟拇指比。

小不點兒瘦又小，
「拇指湯姆」是綽號。
人雖小，膽氣豪，
劍頭鋒利常出鞘；
他曾鼓足一口氣，
戳死蒼蠅三隻命歸西。

打完蒼蠅大事畢，
伏臥打盹他休息。

A raven on his walk near by
Detected him with his sharp eye.
He thought: "A beetle, a strange kind?"

走來一隻大烏鴉，
炯目見他地上趴。
烏鴉以為是怪蟲，

And plucked and tugged him from behind.

一口叼住屁股拖出樹叢。

But Tom's reaction was quite quick,
He gave the bird's leg a sound prick.
The raven laughed: "That was quite good!
But so is also my thick boot!"

湯姆反應不算遲，
拔劍便往烏鴉腿上刺。
「好劍法！」烏鴉呵呵笑，
「但我穿厚靴你可知道！」

He snatched him and soared up to take
The little boy across the lake.

烏鴉抓起他高飛，
小不點俯瞰湖面腳下移。

His parents asked: "Where might he stay,
To be from home so long away?"
They searched for him in bags and hoods,
In bottles, cups, in flasks, and boots.
They called: "Oh, ducky, where are you?
Oh, dearie, come, what shall we do?"

爸媽急得嗷嗷叫：
「他久久不回原因是哪條？」
翻箱倒篋到處搜，
可藏身處全不漏。
「小乖乖，你在哪裡？
小親親，我們怎麼去找你？」

The raven with Tom Thumb, however,
Flew up a tree, higher than ever.
And then he said: "Dear Tom, good-bye",
And slowly on his way did fly.

烏鴉飛落在一樹頂，
棄下「拇指湯姆」高枝停。
　「再見吧！小朋友，」
說完逕往遠處飛去慢悠悠。

Ugh! in a knothole with loud howl
There perched a fearful ugly owl.

喔唷！忽聽得耳邊啼聲淒厲，
貓頭鷹惡狠狠，藏在樹洞把身棲。

Above him a fat crawling spider
Did not for Tom mean much good either.

上方爬來一隻大蜘蛛，
湯姆腹背受敵無出路。

Before the owl could try a trick,
Tom killed the spider with one prick.

不待貓頭鷹發難，
湯姆刺死蜘蛛求生還。

He used its web, came to the ground,
So Tom for now was safe and sound.
Hurrah! down in the mossy ring,
There was a party in full swing.

攀緣蛛網作繩梯，
湯姆平安下了地。
萬歲！樹下一圈苔蘚青，
眾客聚會忙宴飲。

Three merry beetles there drank mead,
Its quality was best indeed.

三隻甲蟲醉醺醺，
蜂蜜酒果然味兒醇。

Three cheers! good health! cried the whole band,
And Tom drank more than he could stand.
His head got dizzy and he wobbled,

「乾杯，乾杯，再乾杯！」甲蟲齊聲勸，
湯姆盡興把酒灌。
頭重重，腳輕輕，

Onto his back he headlong toppled.

仰天一跤跌發昏。

The chafers had a lot of fun,
When they now to an anthill run.

金龜子們取樂忙，
湧往蟻穴去顛狂。

Such places make a man alive,
Be it an anthill or a hive.

蟻穴蜂窩捅不得，
醉酒猛醒湯姆駭。

He ran out of this swarming maze,
And found with joy a sheltering case.

趕緊飛奔逃之天天,
喜見有個藏身袋套。

"Well", said the hunter, "I must go",
Put on his glove and cried : "Oh no!

袋子原是獵人手套，
伸指入套獵人驚叫。

What nasty prick is there, oh fie!"
The hunter yelled out with a cry.

「什麼討厭的扎手貨！」
獵人放聲怒咋呼。

Tom also had some worries here,
And so preferred a mousehole near.
A thief! - a thief! the mouse did shout,
And from behind, Tom was pulled out.

一波未伏一波起，
湯姆鑽進鼠洞把禍避。
老鼠大喊「捉賊囉！」
咬住湯姆屁股往外拖。

A sudden crow! - What does that mean?
The raven came upon the scene.
And when he grabbed the longish tail,
With mouse and Tom did upwards sail,

呱呱一聲啼 ——
老鴉返回出事地。
一口叼住長鼠尾，
拖著老鼠和湯姆衝天飛。

The hunter called: "Now wait a bit!"
And bird and mouse, the two were hit.

獵人看見端槍瞄，
一舉擊中鼠和鳥。

Tom, raven, mouse, for goodness' sake!
Fell headlong down into the lake.

哎喲喲，不得了！
栽進湖水怎麼是好。

But Tom, in great and utmost need,
Met Zephyr, Queen of all the reed.

This princess whispered with great glee:
"My prince, will you my sweetheart be?"

"Great thanks, my Queen, this cannot be,
Because my parents wait for me."

落水湯姆命垂危，
幸好遇上蘆葦女神「和風美」。

女神柔聲喚情郎，
問他可願把駙馬當？

「多謝女神搭救恩，
只因雙親等我回家難從命。」

Then let me come, it's not so late,
My little boat waits at the gate!"

While sailing on the water there,
A lovely and a happy pair,

「那由我隨夫君還，
門口停有小遊船！」

小船悠悠水上游，
好一對親愛小倆口。

Up came a greedy pike, and splash!
Devoured both up in a flash.

貪得無饜的大狗魚，
竄出水面一口把人船都吞去。

An angler soon, however, took
The pike from water with a hook.

溪邊垂釣翁，
釣起狗魚供人烹。

Before he went to fish another,
He brought the pike to Tommy's mother.

They cut the belly with a shout,
For who with glee came striding out?

狗魚送到湯姆母親手，

夫婦剖膛嘆稀有。

喜孜孜從魚膛走出小人一雙，

'Twas our Tommy elegant,
Leading his princess by the hand.

正是牽著女神玉手的我家好兒郎。

And they became a pretty pair,
Lived many years, were happy there.
Tom Thumb became a ladies-tailor,
And what he made was without failure.
He always sewed the clothes with pleasure,
And with a ladder he took measure.

天造地設賢伉儷，
和和美美長相依。
「拇指湯姆」裁衣忙，
匠心巧手人共賞。
縫紉工作最合意，
只是量衣時他得登扶梯。

The Prudent Eagle-Owl

難開金口的貓頭鷹

The eagle-owl is not disturbed,
When others in dispute are heard.
So once a stork and a black raven
Were in dispute, what God in heaven
Had first created: egg or bird.

別的鳥兒大吵鬧，
唯有貓頭鷹不受騷擾。
白鶴烏鴉爭得兇：
要問天上造物主，
首先製造蛋或雛。

The stork was sure: "Of course the bird!
On that we need not waste a word."
The raven croaked "It was the egg,"
And stiffened there upon his neck.

白鶴回答最肯定:「自然是雞先!
這還用得著爭辯!?」
烏鴉扯著破嗓叫:「先有蛋!」
挺著脖子擺橫蠻。

Two frogs in their green jacket
Took sides and thus they quacked it:
The one did croak: "The stork is right."
The other took the raven's side.

兩隻青皮蛙,
也來辯高下。
「我說白鶴對。」一蛙聲粗嗄,
另一蛙附議的是烏鴉。

"What?"– cried the two, still in dispute,
"What nasty, cheeky, croaking hoot?"
Their quarrel ceased, when from the bog.
Each one could relish his own frog.

「哈？」兩鳥爭論不休齊聲問，
「哪個厚臉皮發出難聽沙啞聲？」
說著伸嘴向水塘，
各自叼起一蛙去品嚐。

The eagle-owl, in his dark coat,
Thought, well, I know, and cleared his throat.

披身黑羽貓頭鷹，
自問無所不知清嗓音。

obin Redbreast on the tree,
Wip wip!
Has plucked a berry, as you see,
Nip nip!
And to the water in a wink,
He flies to get a drop to drink,
Stip stip nip nip!
Then soars up to the lilac's pink.

He chirps and sings
With lovely rings,
Zip zip, zip zip
And in his feathers hides his head,
Thus finds a warming slumber bed.

紅胸知更樓樹上，
嘰嘰！
叼來莓果新鮮嚐，
嘻嘻！
霎時鳥兒雙翅展，
飛下枝頭嬉水邊。
唧唧— 嘻嘻！
飲水既畢重向百合高枝返。

唧唧噥噥輕唱啾，
婉轉嘹亮啼聲悠。
嘰嘰，嘰嘰——

一曲唱完去低頭，
胸羽作床好享受。

The Hollow Tooth

蛀牙

A meal may be completely marred
By biting scraps extremely hard.

吃飯咬上砂粒磕，
倒霉透頂崩大牙。

This was the case with Frederik Creek;
He crouches here and holds his cheek.

克利克碰上這種倒霉事，
只好呆坐捧著腮幫子。

One tooth is hollow, this is plain,
To bite on it gave him much pain.

顯然有顆牙蛀空，
咬上硬物鑽心痛。

Some people say the smoke will soothe
The awful pains caused by a tooth.

有人說，抽口煙，
緩解牙痛最靈驗。

His woe gets worse and worse indeed,
He takes some whisky in his need.

當他痛得難忍受，
取來威士忌喝一口。

He dips his head with all his pain
Into cold water, but in vain.

疼痛難禁無法治療，
頭浸涼水一樣無效。

By this he finds but little cheer,
He tries another method here.

上天入地都無門，
他用新法解鬱悶。

And troubled by this dreadful woe,
Inflicts his wife here with a blow.

痛苦惹得他性起，
棒打老婆出惡氣。

A plaster, fixed behind his ear,
Will hardly help, as you see here.

耳朵後面貼膏藥，
照樣痛得直跳腳。

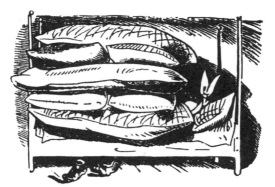

But now he has the inspiration
To try a bath of perspiration.

走投無路心生計，
發身大汗求轉機。

The heat is great, he starts to cough,
And quickly kicks his bed-clothes off.

熱得發暈狂咳嗽，
猛踢被蓋好難受。

89

And struggling with his feet
He weeps in his great need.

雙腳朝天抱頭縮，
呼天搶地他號哭。

Below his bed and on his chest,
Poor Frederik lies, but finds no rest.

鑽到床下肚貼地，
劇痛纏身無躲避。

At last, he now makes up his mind,
Goes where he can the doctor find.

克拉克終於下決心，
去找醫生訴病情。

"How do you do, good Mr. Creek,
I see you have a swollen cheek."

「克拉克先生你好，
看你臉頰腫得高。」

"Of course, no doubt, I bet my boots,
The tooth is hollow in the roots."

「你的病情確不輕，
蛀牙已經爛到根。」

"Well", says the doctor, "if you please",
The peasant does not feel at ease.

醫生說著要動手，
農夫忐忑在心頭。

The doctor smiling gets his tool,
The peasant trembles on his stool.

醫生笑取器械在手，

坐等拔牙，病人渾身抖。

His shock was dreadful, I must tell,
To see the hook he knew so well.

鉤子尖利顯眼前，
病人精神受熱煎。

The doctor now, with calm and skill,
Begins his work the pains to kill.

醫生鎮定又熟練，
拔牙手術似等閒。

While Frederik Creek lets things adrift,
Unconciously he feels a lift.

騰雲駕霧似夢中，
克利克猛覺人體聳。

A sudden jerk, a little shout,
Look here, the nasty tooth is out!

猛扭動，失聲叫，
瞧這蛀牙拔出了。

Amused, relieved, and full of glee,
Creek feels himself of all pains free.

愉快輕鬆咧嘴笑，
克利克病痛立時消。

With dignity, as you can see,
The doctor here receives his fee.

醫生端架子，只把手一攤，
診金付託他包攬。

And Mr. Creek, relieved from pain,
Enjoys his supper here again.

牙病治療食慾開，
克利克美美吃飯菜。

99

The Hostile Neighbours

仇鄰

Between this painter and musician,
The wall is but a thin partition.

畫家樂師居貼鄰，
中間僅隔一薄屏。

To be with sounds in constant touch
Was for the painter's mood too much.

咿呀琴聲永不停，
畫家創作心不寧。

He closed his ears, thus to avoid
The sounds by which he was annoyed.

為阻琴聲求太平，
掩住雙耳拒噪音。

But such a genuine flageolet
Digs through his ears, he creeps to bed.

豈料對方奏起豎笛曲，
尖聲撕耳唯有躲進床下去。

His plan to take revenge is ripe,
And for this purpose finds his pipe.

畫家心生報復計，
找來水管當武器。

The water trickles on the cello,
"Good gracious", cries alarmed the fellow.

嘩嘩水流沖刷大提琴，
　「老天爺！」樂師見狀遂大驚。

And craving for his neighbour's doom,
He rushes to the painter's room.

樂師衝進畫家家，
　恨不得一把掐死他。

Bang! through the canvas in a crash,
He grabs the painter in a flash.

砰！畫布撞出大破洞，
扭住畫家不放鬆。

They struggle fiercefully and hard,
The poodle eagerly takes his part.

仇鄰拚命大打出手，
參戰的還有鬈毛狗。

Though drenched with siccative all right,
The cellist perseveres to fight.

披頭蓋腦全是顏料，
提琴樂師仍不饒。

At last they are fed up with fighting,
The dog enjoys his prey by biting.

筋疲力竭終於罷兵，
留下小狗猶在撕咬戰利品。

Oh Music, you have done this ravage,
And, what was left was dreadful damage.

喔，音樂之神，都怪你，
留下這攤破東西。

Fred On The Donkey

弗雷德騎驢

The pretty girls asked and cried:
"Oh, cousin Fred, do take a ride."

美貌表妹齊聲求：
「哥啊，騎驢遛一遛。」

Fred, being full of readiness,
Wins donkey's mood by friendliness.

弗雷德踴躍充好漢，
調弄頑驢靠友善。

Though straddling well he cannot start,
The cousins laugh: "Oh bless my heart."

騎姿優美，驢卻不行，
表妹齊笑真要命。

Fred said: "Come on and do not fail,
What I must do is turn your tail."

弗雷德好焦躁：

「絞你尾巴準保你快跑。」

To get him finally on the track,
He burns poor donkey on the back.

為使畜生聽擺布，
竟用煙頭去燒驢屁股。

The animal jumps up to bolt,
While Fred's arms hope to get a hold.

驢子受驚狂竄奔，
弗雷德雙臂亂舞抓韁繩。

For gardening there hang many a tool,
And here the donkey plays the fool.

轉眼來到園藝工具棚，
蠢驢在此蹄亂蹬。

The hot house glasses now are smashed,
When donkey's croup against them crashed.

溫室牆撞上蠢驢臀，
玻璃塊塊成齏粉。

The aloe is not sitting place,
The pains you see on donkey's face.

更有龍舌蘭一盆，
刺得驢子呲牙疼。

Pricked by the thorns, with pains half dead,
They drive poor donkey then ahead.

尖齒入肉痛反鈍，
驢子撒蹄又狂奔。

To get a hold Fred is unable,
So he is jerked against the table.

弗雷德雙手失控被拋起，
一頭栽往野餐席。

And upside down with bang and flop,
With butter, milk, and cream on top.

呼呼——嘩啦，桌翻斗，
黃油牛奶盡澆頭。